THE CLONE WARS™

THE NEW PADAWAN

Adapted by Eric Stevens

Based on the movie *STAR WARS: THE CLONE WARS*

P9-CFR-039

Grosset & Dunlap • LucasBooks

GROSSET & DUNLAP
Published by the Penguin Group
Penguin Group (USA) Inc., 375 Hudson Street, New York, New York 10014, USA
Penguin Group (Canada), 90 Eglinton Avenue East, Suite 700,
Toronto, Ontario M4P 2Y3, Canada
(a division of Pearson Penguin Canada Inc.)
Penguin Books Ltd., 80 Strand, London WC2R 0RL, England
Penguin Group Ireland, 25 St. Stephen's Green, Dublin 2, Ireland
(a division of Penguin Books Ltd.)
Penguin Group (Australia), 250 Camberwell Road, Camberwell,
Victoria 3124, Australia
(a division of Pearson Australia Group Pty. Ltd.)
Penguin Books India Pvt. Ltd., 11 Community Centre, Panchsheel Park,
New Delhi—110 017, India
Penguin Group (NZ), 67 Apollo Drive, Rosedale, North Shore 0632, New Zealand
(a division of Pearson New Zealand Ltd.)
Penguin Books (South Africa) (Pty.) Ltd., 24 Sturdee Avenue,
Rosebank, Johannesburg 2196, South Africa

Penguin Books Ltd., Registered Offices:
80 Strand, London WC2R 0RL, England

This book is published in partnership with LucasBooks, a division of Lucasfilm Ltd.

Library of Congress Cataloging-in-Publication Data is available.

ISBN: 978-0-448-44994-4   10 9 8 7 6 5 4 3 2 1

GLOSSARY

Here are some Clone Wars terms that might help you along the way.

Blaster: The main weapon used in the galaxy.

Clone troopers: Identical soldiers bred and trained to serve in the Galactic Republic's army.

The comm: Short for communication system. It's how people talk from ship to ship or from ship to planet.

Destroyer droid: A droid that can transform into a wheel and roll about.

Droid: A robot or android.

Energy shield: A protective barrier made of energy.

The Force: An energy field created by all living things. It gives the Jedi their power.

Galactic Republic: The government that rules the galaxy.

Hologram: A projected image of a person.

Jedi: Masters of the Force. They use their power to protect the Republic.

Jedi Council: The group of twelve Jedi Masters who oversee all the Jedi in the galaxy.

Jedi Temple: The Jedi Temple is the home of the Jedi. It's where they meet and train.

Lightsaber: The weapon of a Jedi. It looks like a sword made of colored energy.

Octuptarra droid: A droid that has long legs and a large head. It has the ability to turn around quickly, which makes it hard to defeat.

Padawan: A young Jedi in training.

Separatist Alliance: The group trying to take over the Galactic Republic.

Togruta: People from the planet Shili.

Youngling: A child who might one day become a Jedi.

PROLOGUE

The Republic is at war! Supreme Chancellor Palpatine, the head of the Galactic Republic, has committed thousands of clone troopers to fight the Separatist Alliance. As planets choose sides, the galaxy is divided. Only the Jedi can keep the Republic from falling apart. Jedi generals Anakin Skywalker and Obi-Wan Kenobi lead the fight against the Separatist Alliance's droid army on the planet Christophsis.

CHAPTER 1

"We're in trouble," Anakin Skywalker said, drawing his lightsaber. Battle droids and spider droids approached, laying down blaster fire as they moved. Anakin blocked several shots and backed toward Obi-Wan Kenobi.

"I knew this victory was too easy," Obi-Wan said, drawing his lightsaber as well. "We never should have sent the ship back for supplies." Several more shots came at them, which Anakin and Obi-Wan easily blocked.

The droid front line was closing. In minutes, the Republic Army would be outnumbered.

Anakin laughed. "It wasn't my idea to send the ship back!" he said.

As the droids reached Anakin and Obi-Wan, the two Jedi swung their lightsabers. One after another the droids were sliced in half, each falling to the ground in two. But it wasn't enough. The droids kept coming.

"There's just too many of them!" Anakin shouted over the noise.

Suddenly, the attack stopped.

"The droids are regrouping," Obi-Wan said, extinguishing his lightsaber.

"Don't get comfortable," Anakin said, pointing down the road. It was littered with wrecked droids, but another wave of attackers was rolling right over them. The new droids started blasting. "They're starting to move again!"

"New plan," Anakin said to Obi-Wan as he deflected blaster fire. "We split up."

Anakin spun, blocked another shot, and called to a clone officer. "Rex! Have your men follow me!"

Obi-Wan watched him go and then turned to the remaining clone troopers. "Battle positions! Commander, at my side. We'll take them directly."

"Yes, sir," Clone Commander Cody replied.

"Positions!" he called back to his men.

"It seems like there are more droids in each wave of attack!" one clone trooper called out.

Obi-Wan, at the front of the Republic's force, looked over his shoulder and waved the troopers onward.

Cody got to his feet and led the charge at Obi-Wan's back. The troopers followed.

Obi-Wan suddenly spotted an octuptarra droid

moving up from behind the enemy line. Its round head rose up above the droids as it fired blast after blast. The Jedi Master crouched into battle position. After a moment, he sprang into the air toward the big, eight-legged droid.

With one slash of his lightsaber, Obi-Wan sliced the octuptarra droid in two, landing beside it. Cody knelt beside him, and for a few moments they were safe behind the destroyed droid.

"General Skywalker should have started his attack by now," the commander said, out of breath. "They've got us pinned down!"

Obi-Wan peeked out around the droid. Blaster fire struck close, and he quickly pulled his head back. "He knows the plan," he replied to the commander. "Don't worry."

Meanwhile, high atop a half-destroyed building, Anakin Skywalker watched as the battle raged on. At his side were several clone troopers, waiting for his signal.

"What's our plan of attack, sir?" one of them asked cautiously.

Anakin stood up and smiled. "Follow me." And with that, he leaped from the rooftop, tumbled once in midair, and grabbed onto the long neck of an octuptarra droid. He hung from the metallic neck as droids fired at him from all directions. Deflecting blast after blast, the Jedi waited for the right moment. Then, with a quick slash of his lightsaber, he sliced through

the droid. A second later, he landed safely on the ground. The clone troopers were at his side in a moment.

They were now behind enemy lines and behind the backs of the droids.

"This way!" Anakin shouted and pointed back toward the front line. They charged from behind the droids, taking them by surprise.

"Push through!" the young Jedi called to the clone troopers at his side. Soon they reached Obi-Wan Kenobi. But the droid numbers were still overwhelming.

"We're surrounded," Anakin said to his old Master. The two crouched together at the center of the raging battle. They deflected blast after blast. Clone troopers continued to defend as best they could, but many were falling. "We need reinforcements!"

Suddenly, the battle droids and spider droids lowered their weapons and turned around.

"They're retreating," Anakin said.

"I wonder why . . ." Obi-Wan began, but Rex interrupted him, grabbing his sleeve.

"Look!" he said, pointing overhead.

The Jedi looked up and saw a single Republic shuttle flying overhead.

"Looks like help has arrived," Obi-Wan said.

CHAPTER 2

Anakin, Obi-Wan, and Captain Rex watched as the shuttle landed in the center of City Plaza.

"Our cruiser must be back," Obi-Wan pointed out.

Anakin nodded. "That means we'll be able to get our reinforcements."

Obi-Wan walked toward the shuttle. "It looks like all of our problems are solved. Fresh troopers, new supplies, and perhaps they brought my new Padawan with them."

Anakin stopped short in surprise. "You really think it's a good idea to bring a Padawan learner into all this?" he added, waving his arms at the destruction around them.

"I spoke to Master Yoda about it. He agreed," Obi-Wan insisted. "You know, Anakin, you should put in a request for your own Padawan. You would make a good teacher."

Anakin chuckled. "No thanks. I don't need some Padawan around, annoying me and needing my help all the time."

"Anakin," Obi-Wan went on, "teaching is a privilege. It's part of the Jedi's responsibility to help train the next generation."

"Not for me," Anakin replied as they reached the bottom of the shuttle ramp. "A Padawan would just slow me down."

A single figure came down the ramp and made her way toward the two Jedi. The young Togruta girl appeared tiny compared to the massive

battle going on around her.

"Who are you supposed to be?" Anakin said with a smirk, leaning down.

The girl stood up straight. "I am Ahsoka. Master Yoda sent me. I am to let you both know that you must return to the Jedi Temple at once."

"Must we?" Anakin said.

"At once?" Obi-Wan asked.

Ahsoka nodded. "There's an emergency."

Anakin chuckled. "Well, maybe you haven't noticed, but we've got a nice little emergency of our own right here."

"That's right," Obi-Wan added. "We've been calling for help. We were rather hoping you might be that help."

"Master Yoda hadn't heard from you, so he sent me to deliver the message," Ahsoka replied.

"Our communications have been unreliable," Obi-Wan explained.

"Great," Anakin said, throwing his hands up and turning around. "They don't even know we're in trouble!"

"Well," Ahsoka pulled a hologram communication disk from her pocket, "maybe you can relay a signal through the cruiser that just dropped me off."

CHAPTER 3

"I have Master Yoda," the clone
communication chief signaled to Obi-Wan Kenobi
from the cruiser above the planet. "However, we
are under attack and I don't know how long we
will be able to maintain orbit, General."

Obi-Wan, Anakin, and Ahsoka watched as
Yoda's image appeared before them.

"Master Kenobi," Yoda said, "glad Ahsoka
found you, I am."

"Master Yoda," Obi-Wan replied quickly,

"Ahsoka gave us your message."

"Yes," Yoda said, nodding. "Come back to the Jedi Temple, you must."

"We are in no position to go anywhere or do anything, Master Yoda," Anakin replied. "Our support ships have all been destroyed."

Yoda wrinkled his face thoughtfully. "Send reinforcements to you, we will."

Suddenly, Yoda's image vanished, and in his place stood the clone communication chief aboard the cruiser.

"General Kenobi, we've lost communication," the clone chief said. "We have to leave orbit immediately. More Separatist warships have arrived."

With that, the hologram fizzled away completely.

"I guess we can hold out a little longer," Anakin said with a shrug.

Obi-Wan nodded and turned to the young

Togruta. "My apologies, young one. It is time for proper introductions."

Ahsoka stood as tall and straight as she could, and said, "I am Ahsoka Tano, the new Padawan learner."

"And I," the older Jedi said, "am Obi-Wan Kenobi, your new Master."

Ahsoka bowed, but then straightened and said, "I am at your service, Master Kenobi, but I'm afraid I've been assigned to Master Skywalker."

"What?!" Anakin said, shocked. "No, no, no. There must be some mistake."

Obi-Wan nodded and frowned at Anakin. "Hmm."

"'Hmm'?" Anakin snapped. He turned to Ahsoka. "He's the one who wanted a Padawan. Not me!"

"Master Yoda was very clear," Ahsoka replied. "I am assigned to Anakin Skywalker, and he is to

supervise my Jedi training."

Anakin shook his head and laughed a little.
"That doesn't make any sense."

"Enough," Obi-Wan interrupted, raising both
his hands. "We will sort this out later. It won't be
long before those droids realize this shuttle was
nothing to fear."

Anakin sighed. "Fine, I'll check on Captain
Rex and the lookout post."

He turned to leave, but Obi-Wan stopped him.
"Eh, Anakin, hadn't you better take her along?"

Anakin rolled his eyes, but waved the girl on.
"Come on," he said as he walked quickly away.

Ahsoka hurried along after her new Master,
happy to be included.

CHAPTER 4

"This way," Anakin said to Ahsoka as the two climbed the steps to the top of a damaged building. "We've been using these abandoned skyscrapers as lookout towers."

"Good plan," Ahsoka replied as she jogged at his side.

"Please," Anakin added, "try not to get in the way."

"What's the status, Rex?" Anakin said as they reached the top.

"Quiet for now, sir," Rex replied. "But it looks like they're gearing up for another assault." He glanced at Ahsoka and cocked his head. "Who's the youngling?"

"I am Ahsoka Tano," she replied. "Master Skywalker's Padawan."

Rex smiled and turned to Anakin. "Didn't you say you'd never have a Padawan, sir?"

Anakin shook his head. "There's been a mix-up. This is General Kenobi's youngling, and we'll get it settled, I promise."

Ahsoka stomped one foot and the two men turned to face her. "Stop calling me youngling," she snapped. "And Master Yoda did not make a 'mix-up.' You're stuck with me, Skyguy, so you better get used to it!"

Rex threw his head back and laughed. "She's a spitfire, isn't she?"

Anakin, though, wasn't amused. "What did you just call me? Don't you get snippy with me, little one. You know, I don't even think you're old enough to be a Padawan!"

"Hmph," Ahsoka replied. "Maybe I'm not, but Master Yoda thinks I am."

"Well, Master Yoda isn't here," Anakin snapped. "I am! So if you think you're ready to train to be a Jedi, you better start proving it."

The young Jedi stood up straight and waved at Captain Rex. "Rex here is going to demonstrate how a little respect can go a long way. You're going to go with him on his rounds to check all the lookouts."

"She is?" Rex said.

Anakin glared at him.

"I mean, she is," the captain corrected. "Right." He slung his blaster rifle over his shoulder and nodded at Ahsoka. "Come on then, youngling."

Ahsoka's shoulder sagged as she followed after him, mumbling, "Padawan."

Captain Rex and Ahsoka made their way along the ruined city streets.

Ahsoka gestured back toward an artillery placement. "Have you thought about moving that line back, Captain? They'd have better cover."

Captain Rex glanced back. "Thanks for the suggestion, but General Skywalker thinks they're fine where they are."

Ahsoka looked at her feet a moment, then clasped her hands behind her back. She looked up at the captain. "So," she said, "if you're a captain, and I'm a Jedi, then technically, I outrank you . . . right?"

Rex laughed. "Technically, you're a youngling."

"Padawan!" Ahsoka snapped.

"Fine, either way," Rex replied. "But in my book, experience outranks everything. Know what I mean?"

Ahsoka thought about it a moment, then nodded. "Well, if experience outranks everything, I guess I'd better get some, huh?"

Rex smiled at her. "Yup, a spitfire."

Just then, a flash of orange light caught Ahsoka's eye. "What's that?"

Rex turned and saw a huge, orange dome of

light far across the city. His face fell. "That is bad news."

"For us?" Ahsoka asked.

Rex nodded. "The Separatists have got an energy shield. That's going to make things nearly impossible."

As the captain and the young Padawan watched, the energy shield began to expand into a larger and larger dome on the horizon.

"Well, little one," Rex said, "you wanted experience? You're about to get plenty."

CHAPTER 5

"Have you seen the energy field?" Rex said as he and Ahsoka walked into the communication station. Anakin and Obi-Wan were standing over a hologram map of the city.

Anakin nodded. "The generator is here," he said, gesturing to the map. "And the shield is growing."

"That's right," Obi-Wan added, "and the droids are moving in, just behind the shield's line."

"Our cannons will be useless against that energy shield," Captain Rex said.

Obi-Wan pointed at the edge of the city, where there were more buildings and narrower streets. "As the droids get closer," he said, "we might try to draw them into the buildings."

"Which would make it harder for them to maneuver," Anakin noted.

Rex nodded. "That might level the playing field a bit."

Ahsoka stepped up between the men. "Um, if that shield is such a big problem, why don't we just take it out?"

The three men gave her a hardened look.

"That's easier said than done, Padawan," Captain Rex said.

Anakin smirked. "You know, I agree with her."

Ahsoka smiled, but Obi-Wan crossed his arms and faced his pupil.

"Look, someone has to get to that shield

generator and destroy it," Anakin said. "That's the key."

Obi-Wan smiled and said, "And you two can tiptoe through enemy lines, past hundreds of droids, and solve this problem together."

"Can do, Master Kenobi," Ahsoka replied with confidence.

"Hey!" Anakin said, spinning to face the Padawan. "I'll decide what we can do!"

Captain Rex rolled his eyes as Obi-Wan went on.

"Okay. Rex and I can engage them here," Obi-Wan said, pointing at a built-up area of the map. "Hopefully, that will give you two enough time to get through their lines, undetected. And get to here." He pointed at the generator.

Rex shook his head. "They won't have much time. The droids far outnumber us, and under that shield, our cannons can't help us."

"Not to mention, if the droids reach the cannons and destroy them, we're done for," Obi-Wan added.

Ahsoka nodded sharply. "We'll figure out a way!" she said, grabbing Anakin's wrist. "Come on, Master. Let's go!"

Anakin marched past his Padawan as they exited the communication station. "If we get out of this alive, youngling, you and I are having a talk."

After the two had left, Rex and Obi-Wan gathered the clone troopers and prepared to engage the droid army. Rex stood beside the Jedi and said, "Do you think Skywalker and his Padawan have a chance out there?"

The droids moved closer and Obi-Wan drew his lightsaber. "They better, or we're all doomed."

CHAPTER 6

"So . . . what's the plan?" Ahsoka whispered.

The Padawan and her new Master were on their stomachs, watching as a group of droids marched up the road toward them.

"Oh, now you want me to think of the plan?" Anakin said with a laugh. "I thought you were the one with a plan!"

"No," Ahsoka replied, "I'm the one with the gung-ho attitude. You're the one with the plan."

"Is that right?" Anakin said, cocking his head.

Ahsoka nodded. "You have the experience, right? Which, by the way, I am looking forward to learning from."

Anakin glared at her a moment, then squinted up the road. "First, we need to get behind that shield, then past their tank lines."

Ahsoka looked off to her right. It was totally clear. "Let's just go around, outflank them!"

"That would take too long," Anakin said. "General Kenobi and Captain Rex can't hold the droids off forever."

"Up the middle then? Sneak through?" Ahsoka offered.

"Impossible," Anakin scoffed. "I mean, unless you can turn yourself invisible, or into a droid!"

"All right, fine," Ahsoka said, "you win. My first lesson will be to wait while you come up with the plan."

"Good news, then," Anakin replied as he rose to his feet. "You won't have to wait long. Come on, I have the plan."

"What is it?" Ahsoka said, jumping up.

"Simple. We'll turn ourselves into a droid."

"I feel like an idiot," Ahsoka mumbled. The two were crouching under the remains of a fallen droid. They inched forward slowly, carrying a metal sheet above their heads. From the outside it appeared as if the droid were moving. "We should be fighting these guys," Ahsoka added, "not sneaking around! We're Jedi, aren't we?"

"Well," Anakin said as the orange glimmer of the energy dome passed over them, "their deflective energy shield just passed over us. If you can't cross their lines, let their lines cross you."

"If you say so," Ahsoka said, clearly not convinced.

"Wait!" Anakin suddenly snapped. "Do you hear that?"

A low rumbling was approaching. It grew louder and louder.

"I'll check on it," Ahsoka said, pushing the metal off them.

"No, wait!" Anakin called, but it was too late. A destroyer droid had spotted them. The droid quickly came to a stop in front of them, and before the Jedi could react, it unrolled and started blasting.

"A destroyer droid!" Ahsoka screamed.

"Run!" Anakin ordered. "This way!" And he started running.

"Run?!" Ahsoka answered, pulling out her lightsaber. "Jedi don't run!"

"I said *run!*" Anakin repeated, grabbing the Padawan's sleeve. "That's an order!"

CHAPTER 7

"Why are we running?" Ahsoka asked between gasps for breath. "We'll never outrun a destroyer droid."

The Jedi and his new Padawan kept moving. Every few steps, Anakin looked back over his shoulder. As he watched, the destroyer droid stopped firing as it folded back into its wheel shape and began rolling after them.

"Stop!" Anakin cried, grabbing hold of Ahsoka's arm.

"You just said run!" Ahsoka said, pulling her arm away.

"And now I'm saying stop," the Jedi replied. "So stop!"

They both stopped short just as the rolling droid was closing in on them. The droid stopped and began to open, but before it could attack, Anakin and Ahsoka drew their lightsabers and sliced the droid in half.

Ahsoka took a deep breath and looked at the destroyed destroyer. "Whew."

Anakin nodded at her. "Good. You take direction well. Maybe there's hope for you yet."

Ahsoka smiled proudly. Her Master looked up at the energy shield, then down at the horizon, looking for the generator.

"This way," he said, and the two took off running again.

Before long, Anakin spotted the generator off in the distance. "There it is," he said,

slowing to a walk.

"What are you waiting for?" Ahsoka said. "Let's blow it up!"

"We have to be careful," Anakin replied. He took each step very carefully.

Ahsoka looked around. It was a clear path between them and the generator. "Careful of what?" she said. "Let's go!" And with that she took off running toward the generator.

"No, wait!" Anakin called, but it was too late.

A field of mine droids emerged from the ground and attacked the young Padawan.

"That's what you need to be careful of," Anakin mumbled to himself as he drew his lightsaber and ran to his Padawan's side. "I'll take care of these droids," Anakin said, slashing his lightsaber and taking out three of the mine droids at once. "You get in there and set these detonators." He tossed a bag to Ahsoka.

CHAPTER 8

Ahsoka ran quickly through the small generator building, placing the explosive charges on the generator's control panels and walls. After setting up the last charge, she opened a small panel on its side and flipped a switch. Instantly, all the charges throughout the station began to flash and beep.

With the detonators activated, the Padawan pulled out her lightsaber and ran back outside to help her Master. However, when she arrived, she found him surrounded on all sides by mine droids. Ahsoka paused, looking up at a high wall. It had one small window about halfway up.

She put away her lightsaber and called over to Anakin, "Skyguy, don't move!" Ahsoka then closed her eyes and raised both her arms.

"What are you doing?" Anakin cried out. "Don't do that!"

Ahsoka smiled slightly as the wall began to shake. She was using the Force to pull it down. After a moment it began to crumble and fall.

"No!" Anakin shouted, covering his head with his arms as the heavy wall collapsed on him and the mine droids. A huge cloud of dust filled the air as the wall crashed around him. But when the dust cleared, Anakin was still standing.

"No problem," Ahsoka said, smiling.

Anakin looked around in disbelief. He was standing in the opening created by the one small window. All the droids had been crushed, but

Anakin was safe. He looked at the Padawan.

"You could have killed me!" Anakin protested.

"I knew what I was doing!" Ahsoka replied, crossing her arms. "I just saved your life!"

Anakin shook his head and put up his hands. "Did you set the charges?"

"Yes."

"Then what are we waiting for?" Anakin asked.

Ahsoka shrugged, then pulled the detonator from her pocket and pressed the button.

Behind her, the charges exploded and sent the shield generator sky-high. A moment later, the orange energy dome crackled, fizzled, and then vanished completely.

CHAPTER 9

At City Plaza, Captain Rex and his troop of clones were still fighting, when the energy shield suddenly vanished from above.

"Sir!" a clone trooper called out. "The shield is down!"

Rex gazed skyward and grinned. "Cannons!" he shouted. "Artillery!"

The clone troopers took their positions at the cannons and began firing. In moments, the Separatist tanks were destroyed. The droids surrendered at once.

Near the destroyed generator, Anakin and Ahsoka climbed aboard a shuttle.

"You were reckless," Anakin said to the young Togruta. "You never would have made it as Obi-Wan's Padawan." The Jedi paused for a moment. "But you just might make it as mine."

Ahsoka looked up at her new Master hopefully.

Soon the shuttle arrived at the Jedi transport ship. Obi-Wan Kenobi was already there, and was in conference with Master Yoda. Anakin and Ahsoka joined the two Masters.

"I was explaining the situation to Master Yoda," Obi-Wan said.

Yoda nodded. "Yes. If not ready for a Padawan, you are, then perhaps Obi-Wan . . ."

"Now wait a minute!" Anakin said, interrupting the Master. "I admit Ahsoka is a little rough around the edges, but with a great deal of training, and some patience, she might amount to something."

"Then assigned to you, she is," Yoda said. "Now, some rest for both you young ones."

Ahsoka bowed to the two Masters before leaving the chamber. Anakin turned to leave, but then addressed his former teacher. "You know, something makes me think this was your plan from the beginning."

Obi-Wan only shrugged as his pupil left. Then he turned to Yoda. "Let's hope Anakin is ready for this responsibility."

"Ready he is to teach an apprentice," Yoda replied. "To let go of his pupil, a greater challenge it will be. Master this, Skywalker must."